THE LITTLE RED HEN

An old fable retold by

Heather Forest

Illustrated by

Susan Gaber

AUGUST HOUSE
LittleFolk
ATLANTA

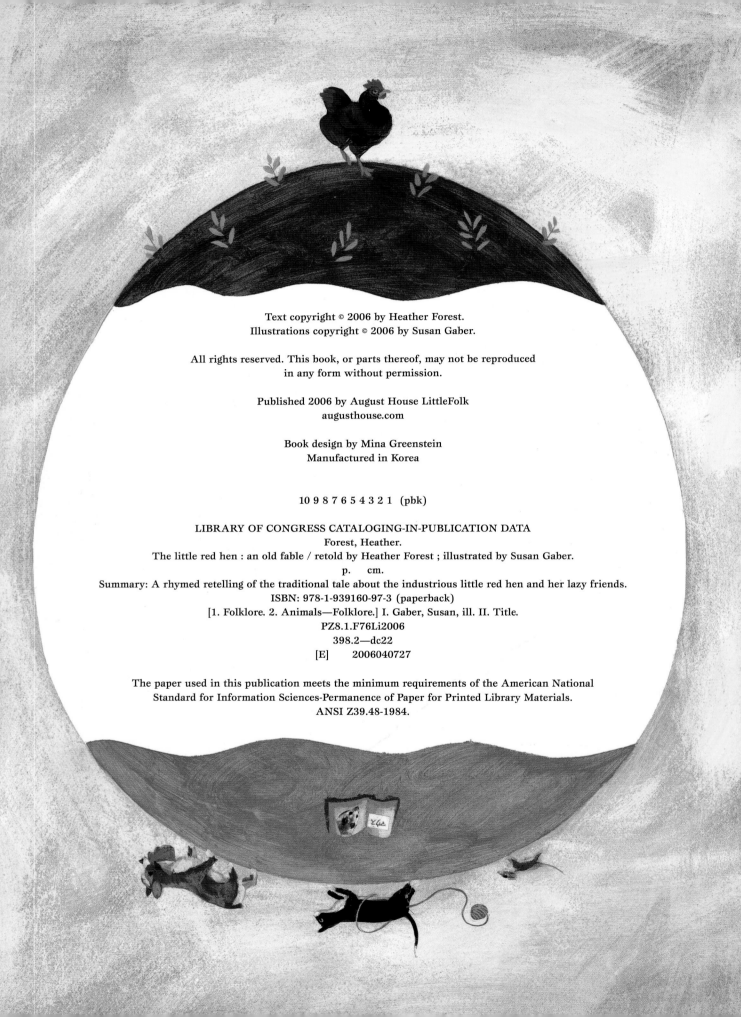

Published 2006 by August House LittleFolk
augusthouse.com

Book design by Mina Greenstein
Manufactured in Korea

10 9 8 7 6 5 4 3 2 1 (pbk)

LIBRARY OF CONGRESS CATALOGING-IN-PUBLICATION DATA
Forest, Heather.
The little red hen : an old fable / retold by Heather Forest ; illustrated by Susan Gaber.
p.   cm.
Summary: A rhymed retelling of the traditional tale about the industrious little red hen and her lazy friends.
ISBN: 978-1-939160-97-3 (paperback)
[1. Folklore. 2. Animals—Folklore.] I. Gaber, Susan, ill. II. Title.
PZ8.1.F76Li2006
398.2—dc22
[E]   2006040727

The paper used in this publication meets the minimum requirements of the American National
Standard for Information Sciences-Permanence of Paper for Printed Library Materials.
ANSI Z39.48-1984.

This book is dedicated to
the seeds of learning.
–HF & SG

ABOUT THE TALE

The Little Red Hen is a popular fable
that has delighted generations of young
listeners and readers since it appeared as a
recommended tale for telling in the 1907
edition of *Stories to Tell Children* by Sara
Cone Bryant, an early advocate for the
art of oral storytelling in libraries
and schools.

A little Red Hen lived in a house,
with a frisky dog, a cat, and a mouse.
One day while she was pecking for worms in the weeds,
she came upon a pile of golden wheat seeds.

She said with delight,
"Dog! Cat! Mouse!
If you'd like some cake to eat,
who will help me plant this wheat?"

The dog said, "Not I."

The cat said, "Not I."

The mouse said, "Not I."

"My, my," said the hen with a sigh,
"I shall have to do it myself."

So the little Red Hen planted the seeds.

She watered them well.

She pulled the weeds.
She tended the plants all alone.

When the stalks had fully grown,
she said with a shout,
"Dog! Cat! Mouse!
If you'd like some cake to eat,
who will help me cut this wheat?"

"My, my," said the hen with a sigh,
"I shall have to do it myself."

So the little Red Hen cut and cut until
she had enough wheat to grind at the mill.
She said with some doubt,
"Dog. . . Cat. . . Mouse. . .
If you'd like some cake to eat,
who will help me grind this wheat?"

The dog said, "Not I."
The cat said, "Not I."

The mouse said, "Not I."

"My, my," said the hen with a sigh,

"I shall have to do it myself."

The little Red Hen ground the wheat to flour.
Then it was the baking hour.
She mixed up the batter and measured so well,
soon the house was filled with a sweet cake smell.

The dog, the cat, and the mouse
followed the scent into the house.

They hungrily admired the handsome treat.
"How delicious!" they shouted. "When do we eat?"

"Alone," the hen replied,

"I planted,

I weeded,

I cut,

I ground

the little pile of golden wheat seeds I found.

Alone, I used the flour to bake.
Now who will help me eat this cake?"

The dog said, "I'll help!"

The cat said, "I'll help!"

The mouse said, "I'll help!"

"My, my," said the hen with a sigh. . .

"I will share my cake with those of you
who help when there is work to do.
For after all is said and done,
working together
makes working fun."

Now. . . .

When the little Red Hen wants to bake,

everyone helps to make the cake,

and everyone helps to eat it.